Seed For The Sower

Seeds Of Truth To Inspire
Spiritual Growth In Everyday Life

Gina R. Burns

Seed For The Sower

ISBN: 9781792844959

CONTENTS

Thank You

How do I say thank you for all you have done? How do I show my gratitude for the love you have shown? How from a pit you delivered me and pulled me up from the miry clay? How you took and cleaned me up by washing all my sins away.

How you out stretched your strong hand and extended it to me wiping all my tears so I could plainly see. How You took my hand in Yours walking together, and showing me Your light – the light to my destiny. How do I even now say thank you for all your yet to do?

I say thank you by always letting my life truly worship you. I say thank you every day by returning that love back to others, giving that love away so freely to others who also need a hand. Showing mercy and kindness to all who are breathing. Continually I say thank you by being Your light to all.

I say thank you by saying, "Yes," to all you have commissioned for me—being that beacon of light and love so others will see You through me. Forever I'll say thank you in all I do and say, and forever we'll be hand in hand as you lead me in Your ways.

Pieces

When my life started out,
it was a blank canvas.
A canvas needing pieces –
pieces that were God-ordained.

Over time I got involved
and added my own pieces.
Pieces that did not fit correctly.
Pieces that were not God-ordained.

Eventually, the canvas became full
although not precisely together.
Outside correctly put together
yet inside mixed and matched.

One day it all fell apart
and the pieces came undone.
The outer edge still intact.
The inside, though, left empty.

Slowly, God-ordained pieces came into place.
Each one fitting correctly together.
Bonded and knitted together as one
so nothing could destroy them.

Each piece feeling the pleasure
of being where it was meant to be.
Each piece bringing hope and joy
of seeing how much God loves me.

To be torn and broken down.
To be yet rearranged.
What a blessing it is
to be put firmly together.

Each piece being God-ordained.

Glue of Love

One by one, they fell – each one to the ground.
Each one hitting the floor harder than the one before.
Every hurt and tear was soon forming a pile.
When I eventually looked down, I saw my shattered heart.

Lying in pieces before my eyes.

Staring at the pieces, I thought, "Could my heart ever be restored,
and did I have enough faith to even believe for it?"
I realized that I was tired and too tired from the pain.
Seeing my shattered heart seemed too impossible to fix.

And yet some hope remained.

While I was looking at the pieces, I saw God also looking on.
He and I seeing together each individual broken piece.
Shortly after, God looked at me and so tenderly said,
Let Me pick them up, daughter – one piece at a time."

"Let My love be the glue that is needed for your heart."

"There are so many pieces, Lord," I said as I looked around.
"Is it possible for all of this to be fully restored?"
My God then carefully picked up the first shattered and broken piece
and held it close to His heart and gave it back to me fully restored.

My eyes watched in amazement and wonder.

My eyes then welled up in tears, not out of sadness though this time
but out of love, hope, and relief that He was there.
Suddenly the process began – one restoration piece at a time.
My God, handling each hurt and tear and giving me back my heart.

Restored completely by His glue of love.

The Garden

One day I took a walk going nowhere in particular. Walking just to walk-free from every worry and care. As I turned the corner, I stopped and looked. There was a clearing that led to a garden, and my eyes then noticed a narrow pathway leading in. As I followed the path, I walked deeper into the garden and saw a garden bench for two. The sun was now casting its rays over this bench. The bench was clothed with the sun coming down from Heaven and was now beckoning me to come, sit and rest. As I took a seat on the bench, I felt the sun warming me, and I started smelling the sweet aroma of the beauty that surrounded me. I then looked around and saw only me. Could it be someone was coming- coming to meet with another? Whose garden is this, I thought, and whose bench is this? To who does all this beauty belong to? Who made this beautiful place? Had I intruded on someone's place? If so, I still couldn't leave. This place was peaceful and so very beautiful. I then felt a gentle touch and a warmth that consumed me. As I looked over, I knew I was not alone.

It was Him – The Master Gardener

His eyes of love met mine, and inside I melted. He said, "Welcome, My Daughter, I've been waiting for you." Here with Me is what is needed. A place for comfort and rest. A place to talk with you and show you, My love. Stay here with Me, Daughter, and rest in My arms. I have so much to tell you- so much to show you."

"That is why I have prepared this place."

I knew at that moment I never wanted to leave. I wanted to live in that beauty and be at rest with Him- The Master Gardener. He knowing my thoughts, said, "You never have to leave." I knew He meant every word, and I vowed to stay forever. Me and The Master Gardener in this beautiful place. A place for Him and me to be forever together. A place free from confusion and worry. A place where dreams come true. A place that He especially created for Him and His Daughter.

The Master Gardener and I

Praying Wives And Mothers

Who will heed the call and become a
steadfast Praying wife and Mother?

Who will fall to her knees on behalf of
her family knowing that the lord for her
will intercede?

Who will be willing to cry out and shed tears
for those who are dear to her heart?

Who in the middle of the night, will lay her hand
upon the ones she loves so dear and believe
her prayers are being heard?

Who will be willing to not grow weary
when her prayers seem to go unnoticed?

Who will persevere knowing God Almighty sees
and recognizes the power of a
Praying Wife and Mother?

Who will give of herself daily to lift her
family up to God? To cry out with her
heart for God's mercy and grace?

Will you be the one who will take a stand
and become a Praying wife and Mother?

Will you rise and answer the call and
then bow upon your knees?

Will you freely give your time
to lift up your family's needs?

Will you rise and answer the call
and be your families voice?

Oh, the power of a Praying Wife and Mother!

A Note From Heaven

I know things have been hard, and you've been grieving. I know how upset you have been that we even had to part. I'm sorry we had to part, and to me, you had to say goodbye. I'm sorry you are now left to only recalling memories. I know you miss me, and your heart is broken. I also know there was so much you had left to say. I have seen your broken heart and the tears you have shed. I have even seen the deep sadness upon your face.

But, Oh, my dear loved one, do not be broken-hearted. For if you could only see all the beauty that surrounds me. To be here in Heaven is a beautiful gift. A gift beyond your imagination and even beyond my description. For I daily walk hand in hand with our Heavenly Father. I see His nail-pierced hands and feet and bask in His warmth and light. I sit and listen to the word coming from His sweet voice. I hear beautiful music playing, and even with angels do I sing. If you only knew what it is like here in Heaven. If you could only see what I see, then you would no longer cry for me.

I know your days at times are hard and lonely. You wonder if I even truly knew how much you loved me. Oh, Yes, I do know of your great love for me, and yet please always remember my great love for you. Know that nothing can keep us apart, for Christ is our eternal bond. So, while it is hard now, know it won't be forever.

We will be together again one day, and it will last for eternity. What a blessing that day will be when we too will be hand in hand. So, for now, though, please smile and with joy remember me. Let your heart be filled with God's love and peace. Fill your days with purpose and carry out His will. He has much for you to do that only you can fulfill. So on this beautiful day, I have been sent to give you a note from Heaven. A note to remind you that you're never alone and that the Heavenlies and I are always looking on.

Looking On With Love In A Note From Heaven

God Almighty

They say God has a plan and that everything happens for a reason. They say everything will work out and to never feel defeated. So why did it all happen, and what does it all mean? Was all the hardship and pain meant to strengthen me, or just the enemy again at work? Are the things of life just life, or is there really a bigger master plan? Is God Almighty really in charge, or are things just left to circumstance?

Looking now back on my situation, I can see how I would have fallen had it not been for God and His strength. I can now see how the enemy attempts to destroy, but how God turns things around for good. I can see that even in my weakness, I'm strong and never defeated. Being now beyond my situation, I see that God does have a plan. I can see that He is in control even in the circumstances I don't understand.

So now, as I look to the future, I realize:

The past is the past, and it is gone. It's to the future that I must now focus and go. Letting go of all the hurt and pain and moving forward in His name. Recognizing I do have a future despite the pain of the past. Taking with me as I go not hurt but lessons. Lessons of who God truly is. Taking those lessons to the streets and offering new hope to others. Hope that offers new life and to life brings purpose. Taking with me the realization that God Almighty truly for each of us has a plan.

Understanding that God is in control and beside us, He'll always stand. Now looking ahead, I can be grateful for that season of weeping. For it is because of that season I found my greatest source of strength.

God Almighty Himself – The Author and Finisher of my faith

My Friend, My Comfort, My Eternal Hope

God Almighty Himself

Commissioned By God

You've endured by knowing whose you are with the helmet of salvation. You've persevered by knowing who you are with the breastplate of righteousness. In the storm, you stood your ground with the shield of faith. In the battle, you had victory with your loins girded with truth. You've dodged the enemy's deadly attempts with the sword of the spirit. Now with your feet shod with the preparation of the gospel of peace:

I hear by do send thee out.

The time has now come for you to finally go. To go and be all that I've pre-destined you to be. To go and set the captives free and bring sight to the blind. To present the gospel of Jesus Christ to every city, state, and nation. To be an example to the world that God is in control and will use anyone who is willing to let go of their own plans. To simply use you as a living testimony of God's mercy and grace.

So now go.

Go in the hope and favor of God and watch what I will do. Watch the souls that will be won by simply saying My name. Go with the reassurance that I'm with you and you are ready. Ready to stand and speak with boldness and confidence, knowing that I put you there. Know that every step you take will be a step that is preordained and that every word spoken will first come from Me.

Go, child. Go forth in Me, and be all that you were created to be. Go and be a light for me. A light that, when it is brought into darkness, brings healing and life. A light that is an eternal reflection of God's mercy and grace. So, go now knowing that by Me, you're commissioned and have My stamp of approval.

Go!

Conversations

To finally be here in the middle of this is almost unbelievable. To see how it has all come together is almost too good to be true. However, You knew the truth all along God because You are the truth and set all this into motion.

They said, "It couldn't be done and that it sounded impossible." You said, "They would all one day know that the hand of the Lord hath done it."

They said, "It would take time and to not think too big." You said, "Time is running out, and you need to go global so everyone can be a part of it."

They say, "Who are you to be here- what qualifies you to be on stage?" You say, "The plan has been set, and you're going to confound even the wise."

I say, "God is all this really true- it's much bigger than even I could have imagined?" You say, "Yes, child, it's bigger and true- now run to it, not away from it."

They now say, "You were right to keep believing in your God-given dream, For God has shown up for you and to the world is showing off."

The others say, "Thank God He is!" The others now come saying, "Thank you for not giving up and for having the faith. Thank you that you didn't give in because we now have a safe place to gather. A place created just for us. A place to experience God and His love. Thank you that you kept the faith and now teach us to do the same."

Now the three-fold cord cannot be broken. God the Father, me the servant, and those who hunger. All three in agreement with each other and willing to walk together.

Despite whatever anyone may say!

The Power of One

Can one person really make a difference and bring change to people's lives? Can one person be enough to light the path for others to walk in? Can one person's love for Christ be enough to ignite a Holy fire? Can even one person's obedience to Christ be enough to lead others in faith?

If you think the answer is no, you need to quickly reconsider: Think to those of long-ago faith who made God's hall of fame. Those who started out as one called and chosen by God. Those who through faith stepped out, so others could step in.

To serve the one and only true God.

You say, "I'm but only one person – how could I inspire faith and change?" Simply put, the answer never lies in because of us, but because of who lives IN us. Every believer has the power within them because of God Almighty Himself. He has filled us with everything we will ever need to bring Him glory.

God, though, never calls the army without first bringing forth that one. That one through Christ will lead knowing that the battle has already been won. Many will then come and follow that lead and will believe. Many will sit back and say, "Thank God for the faith of one." Then they, because of your stepping out, will no longer be afraid to stand boldly and say, "I want to be the next one. The one who will let God use them for His purposes." The one who says, "Use me and send me to help bring forth faith and change."

One person through faith can bring change. One person of perseverance can bring hope. All of this accomplished through the power of God Himself.

Poured out through the Power of One.

A Higher Standard

Who is willing to go all the way for what they believe? Who is willing to take a stand, even if it means standing alone? Who will be willing to raise the bar by not looking like the world? Who will be willing to stay there even if they are left alone?

Too often, we want the blessings, but not the discipline required. Too often, we just want rejoicing without that season of mourning. Too often, we want the favor of God without any personal giving. Too often, we want the gifts, but not the gift giver Himself. Too often, our lives reflect us and only a morsel of God. Too often, we demand God's help and yet refuse self-sacrifice.

We all end up standing for something, whether it's God or not. Each of us daily makes a commitment to either ourselves or to Christ. However, to be in this world doesn't mean we are to look like the world. As children of God, shouldn't we look and act differently? Shouldn't we be setting the standard of a pure and holy life? Shouldn't we also be representatives of freedom from the enemy and his strongholds?

Oh, that one would take a stand and not give in. One who would gladly stand for righteousness and holiness. One who would give their all to be an example of Christ. One who would not conform to be liked or loved by the world?

God is saying to one and all, "Will you be the one? Will you gladly and publicly take a stand and declare it to the world? Will you be the one that will help lead others into a life of holy living? A life that is set apart and used for the glory of God. That life that is sanctified and purified for the cause. That life that is lived out by a higher standard?"

Again, how will the world ever know who God's children are if everyone looks the same? Raise the bar and lift the standard Oh children of the king. Lift your voices and loudly sing, declaring that you are free.

And Live A Life Of A Higher Standard.

Homecoming

Who will we see first on that great day? Who will be the one to give the first hug? Will it be that friend from long ago? That friend who went away before their time?

Will it be that Grandma or Grandpa to give the first hug? Perhaps it will be the two of them together that greet us. Maybe it will be that sweet and dear sister. That one who we desperately miss and with her is the beloved brother.

Then again, will it be that Mom or Dad? The Mom or Dad that when left took a piece of us with them? What if it is that child who went too young? That one who never got the chance to live a long full life?

Most likely, it will be all the above, and yet does it really matter? For the first face we will most likely see is that of our Heavenly Father. The Great and Mighty One- the One who for us has provided everything. He will greet, hug, kiss, and usher us in. Then beside Him is where we will see all those who came with Him to welcome us. We'll see everyone we had lost- everyone we had to say goodbye to. We will, in an instant, be surrounded by everyone who meant the world to us.

On the day that we walk into eternity with our, Lord will be the day of our homecoming. It will be a glorious day- a day of rejoicing and of eternal reunions. An eternity in where tears no longer exist, and sadness of heart is replaced. Forever replaced by the everlasting love of God, family, and friends. A daily eternity of true rejoicing that will never end.

All of this will be on the day that we walk into our
Eternal homecoming!

Faithful

Why do we waste so much time trying to do things our way? Why do we fret and worry when God is in control? Why do we continually try to make things happen ourselves and then lay in bed at night, unable to sleep because of fear?

God tells us to cast our cares upon Him, and yet we don't. God promises His children peace and rest, and yet we don't receive it- why? Perhaps each of us, for a moment, need to reflect on the past. To take that moment of reflection and remember how God has shown up.

To remember how He proved Himself faithful.

God's greatest testimonies are through His children- you and me. Each of us has a story or two to tell. That story that increases hope because of how impossible things seemed at the time. That story that inspires faith because of how God showed up.

And proved again that He is faithful.

Difficult times are never desired but are so needed. For if we never experienced them, how could God truly show us Himself? So, at night when you lay your head down, lie at complete peace and rest. Know that even while you are sleeping, He is still for you working. Know that God never quits or gives up, and He is constantly working on your behalf. He is moment by moment working to again prove that He and His love is forever and completely to you –

Faithful

The Christian

What does it mean to be a Christian, and what does one look like? Is it that person who serves in the church or the person who serves in the streets? Does the Christian gossip, swear, and judge their neighbor next door? Is the Christian that person who turns their head to the needy and poor, or the person who extends their hand to the poor? Does the person with all the right words seem to be the one? What about the person who has the knowledge but doesn't have the deeds? They that supposedly have all the answers, and yet they lack strength and peace.

To look at Christ and see all He did is the example for us all. For He came not to be served, but He Himself came to serve. He healed, fed, encouraged, loved, and brought all to Him. Even He, our Lord, our Christ on His knees, washed the dirty feet. To look like a Christian is one thing; however, to be one is something entirely different. It is to be willing to do unto others as you would have done to you. It's about constant love and forgiveness no matter what the trespass, and speaking only words that bring healing and life. It's about fully letting go of self and living life for Him. It's not about a title or name, but truly about one's heart.

The Christian is one whose whole heart and life belongs to God. That one who knows that without God, they could not survive. The Christian is one who is not perfect but yet strives for excellence. That one who can admit mistakes, repent, and then be led by God's grace. The Christian is one who offers love, faith, and forgiveness freely. That one who is willing like Christ to wash even one's dirty feet. The Christian is an outward expression of God Himself. That one who brings light and hope into a dark and cold world. That person who is spirit-led and not worldly driven, that person who is willing to lay everything down:

For Jesus Christ, their Lord.

Are you that Christian?

What Is Worship?

What is worship, and how does one define it? Is it a few passionate songs sung on a Sunday morning? Is it the big bill that we publicly put into the offering plate? Is it all the hands-on a Wednesday night that we rush in to shake? Is it all about saying "I surrender" and then going home unchanged? Is it even thinking that once or twice a week in God's house is enough?

True and honest worship is about Him and should never be about us. It's about letting go of our pride and goodbye to our agendas. It's about letting God be in control of everything we say, do, and think. It's even about being willing to look different to our friends, neighbors, and never hiding the fact that we believe and serve Jesus Christ. It's about serving others even when it's inconvenient and being willing to extend our hearts, hands, and even at times, our wallets. It's about loving those who at the moment are not lovable and looking for the good when all seems to be lost.

True worship is about saying "Yes" to all God requires of us. Being willing to do whatever He asks, even when we don't think we can. It's about being God's hands and feet to a world that needs hope. It's about being God's voice to a world that needs answers. It's about praising God in heaven when the answer seems to be no and having a grateful heart even when times are tough.

Worship is defined by being able to completely let go of ourselves and being able to see God through life's ups and downs. Worship is trusting. He'll make a way when things seem to be unending. Worship is about that even if God stopped blessing us, we would still fall upon our knees in worship- because God is still God. Worship is a matter of the heart and should ultimately be a lifestyle. Something that takes precedent above any and everything in our lives. To realize that everything we do should be about worshipping God and bringing Him honor and praise. Worship isn't about perfection and always having a great day, but rather it's about our hearts being connected to God in every way. To every day, wake up and say to God, "What can I do as worship unto You today?" What can I do today that will bring You honor and glory because of my love for you?" This is what true worship should sound and look like.

My Everything

Who is it you hear when no one's around? Who is it you run to when everyone else has left? Who is the one listening when others have turned away? Who is the one left holding your hand when everyone else has turned their head? Who is the one that makes things better for you, because they are closer than a brother and stronger than a friend? Who is the one that sees your broken heart and offers to mend the pain? Who is the one that sees your fear and yet somehow pushes you through it?

Who is that one person that can fix everything? That one who is stronger and mightier than any known person or force. That one who in the night sees the tears that are shed and knows the hurt of the painful words that were said? That one who is the strength for you when you feel you are too weak to go on? That one who, when you are struggling, says, "You can do this because I'm here to help you."

That one who knows your every thought and in their perfect timing says, "I love you, and everything is going to be alright." That one who says, "Even though you feel alone right now, know that you're not. Know that I am right here with you." That one who even on your worst day thinks you're are the best and on your best days says, "I am so proud of you."

The one that I'm talking about is my Lord, my everything. Do you know Him? He is my strength, my comfort, my healer, my provider. Truly, He's my best friend. Any and everything I could ever need is provided through Him, and there's not one thing He won't do for you or for me. As I face each new day, I know I am not alone. I know He's with me, and He's never going to leave me. I know that no matter what comes my way, He will handle it, and therefore I need not be afraid. I know I'm forever blessed to have everything and that everything is Jesus.

If you want to know Him as your everything too, all you have to do is ask. Reach out with your heart and voice and call unto Him. Ask Him to come into your heart, your life, and be your everything like I did. Know that He will hear and answer your call and will gladly come in and wash your sins away. Now rejoice, my friend; because of your doing this, you now have all that I have, and that is: Everything.

Faith

What is faith, and what does it look like? Is it wishful thinking or relying on hope alone? Is faith something you can buy, or is it freely given by God? Is faith only for the "Holy" or is it something that is for everyone? Is faith something only needed for certain moments, or is it to be lived out from day to day? Is faith only for the rich and separated by the poor? Does faith have a name or face to it? Is faith found in the possession of things, or is it something you can never find?

Faith is difficult to describe because for each of us, it is different. For some may seem to have that "Holy" faith, while others seem to have none. Some only have faith in themselves, which results in isolation from others. Some have faith only when things are going well, and for some faith is all they feel they have.

True and unadulterated faith is truly about God. That knowing that all things will turn out for good even though at the moment things are rough. The knowing of even though you're in the valley, you know God won't leave you there. Faith is when you can see and believe in something that others just can't. Faith knows and believes what God has said to you even if your circumstances start to dictate "no." Faith is a gift, and it's given by God. Each person was pre-given the exact amount needed, and that will never be taken away. God, Himself, describes faith as being sure of what we hope for and certain of what we do not see. God also tells us that it is impossible to please Him if we do not have faith.

So again, what is faith, and what does it look like? How much faith is required, and how much does one person need? Even though for each of us, it is different, it is still somewhat the same. Faith is simply a matter of believing what your natural mind cannot. Faith is knowing that God is in control and always keeps His promises. Faith believes that through God, life situations are already handled and that His word is always true. Faith is humbly recognizing you don't have the solution or answers, and God's way is the best way even if you do not understand it.

Faith is not the blind leading the blind, but letting God Almighty, Himself lead and guide. Leading and guiding in a way that will ultimately bring Him honor and glory. Faith is basically all we have because to even believe in God requires faith. Faith is a gift, a necessity, and a requirement for each day. Faith is the only road you will ever need to travel because it is the only road that will ever lead you to Christ.

Simply put, faith is what will help you day to day and what will ultimately decide the place of your eternity. Faith is something we all need for many reasons, and even if it's as small as a mustard seed, God says that is enough. We are to each day rely on what is in us, and that is the faith and belief that Jesus Christ lives in us and is always working things out for our best. That knowing we can fully trust God for all our needs no matter how big or small.

This is just the beginning of what faith looks and sounds like.

Be Still

What do you do when God says, "No, not right now?" What do you do when God says, "Be still and know that I am God?" What do you do when God says, "Shh, let Me do My work?" What do you do when God says, "Just sit and watch the glory and honor that I will receive and watch what the world will say because even they themselves did not believe?" What do you do when God says, "Sit down, child. Sit right in the middle of it all, and just wait?" What do you do when you feel like the world is to you a vacuum, and yet God is demanding you to sit and be still?

You do the only thing that you can, and that is to be still and wait. To take your seat humbly and watch what the Lord does best. To sit in the middle of it all, watching Him all around you working. Soon after this, you will see you yourself have changed even if at first, the situation has not. You'll start to notice that the changes had to first take place within you and that humbly sitting with God is where you should have been all along.

Then suddenly, the day will come when you'll start to notice the Holy Wind has begun to pick up. That things have started to move and breathe again, and all around you, things are starting to change-change for the better. Circumstances are no longer the same, just as the people are no longer the same. The hopeless moments of fear and despair have suddenly turned into the greatest joy.

As you start to look around, you will find that being in the middle is different now. You're not being asked to sit and wait anymore; instead, you are now being asked to arise, run, and dance. Your weeping has turned to joy, and the pain has been healed. Your prayers, you now realize, were truly being heard the whole time.

All this taking place because God asked for you to first humbly sit and be still. All of this because of His great love for you.

All of this because you obeyed the Lord by just being still.

Your Chapter

Your life is now beginning a new chapter, and it can only be written by you. You yourself are the author, illustrator, and publisher of each page that you will daily fill. Know that life is a marvelous gift and one to be revered. It can be described many ways, and yet one of the best is that "Life is a journey." It's a journey of new discoveries and, at times, very eye-widening. It can bring pain, but yet there's always healing. It always brings joy and love through nature and others, and just as the seasons change, so will change always be yours.

Your life will be one that will birth many emotions. Times of sheer happiness and bliss, and yet even times of deep sadness. Times of mistakes that were made and often times of right choices. Times that will require deep reflection and moments that demand great faith. Your life each day will begin anew as the sun rises, and each morning that your eyes awake will be to you yet another gift of a new day. A day that can bring change or just enjoying where you are. A day that can be filled with laughter and embracing those around you. A day that can be filled with new possibilities and be exactly what you want it to be.

Live your life one day at a time and yet live it as though it were your last. Understand that even though challenges come, they will also bring out the best in you and that to you, nothing is impossible. Always be willing to take a chance and forever let your heart be loved. Be courageous and strong enough to take a stand for what is right and yet wise enough to admit when you are wrong. Always remember that you and your life are precious, and you will make a difference in this world. Be confident to always pursue your dreams and yet humble at the same time.

May God bless you as you embark on your new journey. May your faith guide you and His love keep you. May you always understand your God's creation, and His love for you is deep. May you always know that even if you feel alone, you're not because of God's promising that He would never leave nor forsake you. Keep your eyes focused on what lies ahead and not on what is behind. Keep running the race, and know you will eventually receive the prize!

Go now and be all you were pre-destined to be. Enjoy your life and fill each page as only you can. May you bring inspiration and hope to those around you, and ultimately honor and glory to your Heavenly maker as you:

Daily Write Your Chapter.

If Only

Why do we give up so soon? Why do we say, "All hope is gone," and think about calling it quits? If only we could see what was around the bend, we would change our minds. If only we could hang on for just a little longer, we would see that the answer was on its way. If only we could truly know that God's strength was enough and that even in our weakness, we are made strong. If only we could quit looking at the storms and just walk on the water, then much more would be accomplished for the glory of God?

We say things like, "It's too impossible, and I've waited long enough," and yet things were never intended to happen on our timing, but in God's. We think our prayers at times are not being heard, much less answered because answers do not happen when we think they should. We get tired from seeing the problem and then feel our hope is misguided, but yet we don't ask for guidance and wisdom to get through it. We actually believe at times that things will always stay the same, and then to others, we claim to have unwavering faith.

Oh, if only we would trust God and believe that for us He is constantly working. If only we wouldn't go by what we see at the moment, but instead live each moment in faith. If only we could just force ourselves to daily press in, then we would see what He really had planned.

For if we kept pressing in on faith, then we would see. We would see that our prayers had been answered and that God in His goodness has rendered to us double. We, in our amazement, would be so happy we didn't quit and relieved that we didn't give in. For then, in the end, the glory of God would be shown, and all would know that God does answer prayers.

If we could only quit trying to make things about our needs and wants, then maybe God could do what He needed to do. However, while God hears and sees our needs, He's also making a way through our situation for others. If only we would let God be God and work things out how He sees fit, then we would very much be in awe. We would be in awe of how much love He has for us and that on us He never quits. Even when we ponder the question, "Should we give up and quit?"

Oh, if only.

Come

Arise, oh Church, and quit sleeping. Stand to your feet, ready to hear the word of the Lord.

Make haste and run to the front line, ready to receive your marching orders. You have said you're the Army, now to you I lay the charge.

I'm commanding and calling all troops to come. Come and stand at attention and ready to receive. Come and be willing to lay everything down for Me.

Come and hear My message for you to preach. Come and heed the call that is placed upon you. Come and stop playing games; for now is the time for battle. Now is the time to see victory in the streets

If you will not now come, you will be overlooked. You will be left wondering, "Why didn't I show up?" Come for My yoke is easy and My burden light- come and pick up your cross and with Me daily walk.

Come and receive your orders, for others are waiting. They're waiting for God's Army to bring them into the light.

Come one, come all and don't delay. Let go of your agendas, pride, and serve the Living God.

Serve Him with all that you are, and then you will walk in the truest light. The light of The Most High.

Come

We The Body

The word says that a house divided against itself cannot stand. So then why do we as the body fight and quarrel over who is right? Why do we insist that our denomination is the only one that is true? One group says this and that while pointing their Holy finger- while another group says others are wrong- that only they know the truth.

Jesus Christ, Himself, is the Son of God and not a form of religion. He Himself is the Way, the Truth, and the Life and not a man-made form of traditionalism. Jesus said to follow Him and to love Him with all that we are. To then turn around and return that love freely back to others. He never said which man-made denomination was the one true way. He said, "Believe in Me and follow My commands, and then you will be saved." He said He went to prepare for us a place in Heaven. A place that is made up of golden streets- not divided by manmade titles. For in Heaven with God, Almighty is where we will all be one- one in Him. We will all be known as His children and not separated by denominations.

So, for the time we each have left, we are to be united. We need to let go of our personal doctrines and follow Christ and His example. We are to get back to the basics and follow Jesus Christ. We are to serve the Living God and break free of our hindering church walls.

We are to be the body of Christ. A body united under God. A body that, when united, is healed and free. A body that can go into this world and accomplish what God has said. A body that brings healing and life and never again destroys itself.

For if we as the body choose to be divided, how will we ever stand? How will we ever reach the lost when it's us who seems to be lost? How can we fully represent Jesus if we're broken into so many pieces? Pieces that have been crushed and broken down by our own selfish selves.

The world needs the body of Christ to bring them healing and life. To bring them out of the darkness so they can freely walk in the light. If we as the body of Christ do not fully come together, someone else will be there to offer darkened and blinded hope. The world is begging for a united body of Christ. Can we meet the need as true representatives of Christ, or are we too busy trying to prove to each other within the body who is right? Either way, time is running out, and Christ is now asking us to let go of our pride and truly be the body of Christ. To be united and reach the world for Him. The only question is:

Will you and I, as the body of Christ, rise and answer the call?

I Choose

Am I willing to go all out for what I believe? Am I also willing to be laughed at for what I believe? Am I willing to be talked about for what I believe? Am I willing to step out in faith for what I believe? Am I willing to take that chance even if others think it's too risky?

The only answer I know is "Yes." For if I don't, I may as well be dead. For to live is to die, and to die is to live. Life without risk and chances is not really living. To be a Christian is to be different. To be a Christ-follower is to even at times appear controversial, at least to the world and the unbeliever.

If I always stand idle, I'm not living. If I always stay parked, I'm also never moving. I need to move and breathe in God. To not take in the breath of this world, for this world only breathes death and destruction. While I'm in this world, I'm reminded I'm not of it. I was created to bring healing, life, and light. I was created for such a time as this, and for this cause, I now live. For this reason, I dare to take a chance. I choose to step out and be different, no matter what others may say. For I know only One voice matters, and that is the voice of the One I follow. The voice of the One who created me and has ordered my steps. The voice of the Most High One. The voice of my Heavenly Father – the voice that is now calling me.

This is the voice of the one I follow, not the eerie and lying voice of the world. Now, because I hear that true voice calling, I go. I step out in faith and take that chance. I take the first step – that step that begins the rest of my life. That step that is God-ordained and to others brings the healing rain.

So, do I choose to be different? Absolutely! For what other choice is there? I choose to now listen, obey, and move. To move forward in all, God has predestined for me. I now choose to live – really live.

For what other choice is there?

The Mountain

Thinking back, I now wonder how many times did I actually walk around that mountain? How with each trip I swore it would finally be my last, and yet around and around I daily went.

What started out as a small thing turned into half of my life. Each trip around that mountain made me more out of breath. Each trip slowly started to take away the core of me. Each time around that mountain brought more shame, guilt, and pain. Why wouldn't I just see there was a better way – a way out?

Then one day, as I stopped and paused from the exhausting and tiring trip, I fell to my knees and boldly said, "I quit!" I bowed my head to God above and said, "Forgive me. I'm done!" I poured out all my fears, pain, sin, and for eternity left them there.

The Lord then gave me the strength to rise again. He showed me the way out – the way to a better life. As I started off again, this time to the Promised Land, I could only grin. I quickly looked behind me at that giant mountain and realized it wasn't that big. I felt renewed and strengthened and ready to begin again.

Although those trips around and around wore me and others out, I'm thankful. I'm thankful for what I have learned and for all that I have seen. I'm stronger, and I'm better, and I'm alive despite the terrain of that mountain. My God lives and reigns, and even there, I was not left alone.

So now the latter half of my life will be better than the former. I will stay rooted and grounded in the land of the fruitful. I will look to the future and not only at the side of a mountain. I will keep my focus on the One I need to follow and let Him be my guide. I will never try to do things my way again, for I know that will lead me around and around that silly ole' mountain.

The Journey of The Storm

One day I got the call to journey across. I got the call that would ultimately change the course of my life forever. I immediately said, "Yes," and quickly started off. As I looked abroad at the sea I wondered what type of journey this would be. I took my oars and diligently armed each hand. I took my comfortable seat and set my sights ahead. As I oared my way across, I noticed some rumblings. I looked above in the sky and saw the dark clouds quickly forming. My thoughts then quickly turned to how far I had yet to go and hoping the rumblings would soon quiet down.

As I got halfway across, I felt the wind severely picking up. The dark clouds were causing me to struggle to see. The raindrops had started one by one to fall. As I struggled to cover myself, I realized time was running out. The storm was now in its fullest, and I seemed to be the target. Every which way the wind was blowing me, so much that I almost inwardly fell. I thought if I only had someone with me – someone to help me row. Never the less I had answered the call and felt it was now up to me to finish the task that I set out to do. I knew then if I gave up, the waters would completely engulf me. The wind would take me, and never again would I be found.

Suddenly, in the midst of my fear, I felt the strength of ten thousand beside me. Each one giving me the power to push through the mighty rushing waters. Each one giving me the desire and strength to reach the other side. At that moment, in the dark, I realized I was not alone. I knew that this was a test – a part of the call that I had said "yes" too. That test to really find out who in the storm I was and who I would eventually become. A time for me to see and know that I'm never defeated or alone. That even in the darkest storm He my Victor is always with me.

So, with the help of Him and the ten thousand, I boldly grinned through the rain. My body physically beaten and tired, yet my spirit divinely energized. We rowed and rowed together until the storm had passed. Then as quickly as it came, it left, and out came the sun. The waters suddenly returned calm and as smooth as glass. As I wiped off my wet face, I then saw the other side. I saw the shore of where I was meant to be. I saw that now I only had to glide in easily. As I looked

I thought for sure I saw the ten thousand for there were so many people. So many people glowing as bright shining lights and cheering for me to come over. I could even hear the faintest noise in the distance as if it were a chorus ringing out in victory. As I once more looked above, I saw this time a colorful rainbow, and then I knew – I really knew it had all along been Him.

As I docked at the shore though, I noticed everyone was gone. It was only me in the flesh that I could now see. I looked at myself all wet and tired and realized still some strength remained. I had made it – made it safely to the other side. I made it to where my destiny was to begin and all because I answered the call.

The storm was not easy or likable but oh so much needed. For how would I have known the strength of Him and His ten thousand? How would I have ever known that He is my anchor? Ultimately, how could I ever help others safely cross if I myself had never gotten in? All of this because of the greatest journey of my life.

The Journey Of The Storm

The Army of The Lord

The trumpet had sounded, and the last few then came. Those who had been called had now also been chosen. As the crowd grew, the rows quickly started to form a straight line. Each person stood at attention, waiting to hear their commanding officer. Each person moved in closer to each other to the one who was also called and chosen. Each person making room available so that no one was left out. As the crowd stood in formation, He, the Commander, stood in the front. He asked that the doors then be shut, for the room He said was now full.

Each person stood in awe and silence and waited for their orders. Each person was now hand in hand alongside their brother and sister. The Commander then spoke out and said, "Thank you for coming and for answering My call. Thank you for trusting in Me and for laying aside everything." Then He smiled at each one with love and tenderness of heart, and without speaking, each of us also knew the other one was thankful to be there.

He then pulled out, one at time, robes of purple majesty. He came to each of us and clothed us with the anointed robes. As He placed the robe around our shoulders, He pronounced publicly to each our call. He then listed the heavenly gifts that were to each one placed. As the last robe was adorned, He then passed out the cords. He placed gold cording around our necks and then proclaimed we were to now go out. He told each one what mission laid ahead and to whom they were called. He informed us as to who would partner with whom, and who would go their own way.

As the last marching order was passed out, He again went to the front. He asked us to bow our heads, and from the Father above, He ordained and blessed us. He then lifted His hands to the sky and asked His Father also for His blessing. He prayed that each of us would fulfill our calling and forever keep our heads upon His altar. He told us that there would be times of hardship, and yet many glorious times as well. He told us we were going into the darkness as His bright and Holy Light.

He also commanded that each gift be used to its humble fullest. That each accolade be first given back to God the Father. He reassured us of our calling and said that in us, He believed. He reminded us that it was for this moment we were each created. He said that real soon, we would again be brought back together. That each of us would to Him, give an account of the gifts that had been given. He said He was looking forward to how many we would also bring back with us. Those that were at one time walking in the darkness, but later chose to walk into the light. He said he would never be far or distant from us and that anytime we felt afraid, we were to call out upon His name.

He called us that day, "The Army – The Army of the Lord." He also gently added that we, as His beautiful children, He Himself was proud. We all then looked at each other with our purple robes topped off with gold cording and grinned. We knew we had made it, for we were now officially the called and the chosen, and now each of us had a job to do – a job in the army.

The Army of The Lord

Masks

Who is the great pretender? Is it you or is it I? Who is the one wearing the mask of "having it all together?" Who is it that awakes each morning and in the mirror puts on their daily mask? That one who doesn't want anyone to know what is really going on deep inside. That one who is barely living because of their choking reality. That one who feels alone because no one is seeing or listening. Some wear masks to cover up while others wear a mask of denial. Some don't want others to know their pasts while others don't want their present exposed.

How did each of us get this way? Who even gave a cause for the invention of the mask? For Christ did not set us free to hand us then a convenient mask. Christ said our sins are forgiven and that in trouble, He would always be there. He said to come to Him as we are, for only He truly knows our hearts.

It is us who has invented the mask – the mask of the ultimate cover-up. We have, by judgment, gossip, and sneers given cause for the mask to appear. We have not allowed ourselves or others to freely be themselves. To recognize people make mistakes, and some are facing real pressing issues. We have collectively handed out masks so that everyone looks the same. We have chosen to look the other way because even we, at times, choose to wear our daily mask.

So, who will be the first one to boldly take off the deceiving mask? Who will be the first to openly speak out for the pain they inflicted and/or endured? Who will be willing to be exposed and to truthfully share? Who then also for them will be willing to be there? Who will be willing to admit their addictions or fears? Who will be brave enough to say, "I know, for I myself have once been there."

Oh, if only they could, one by one, go and be tossed in the trash. Never again to be seen and never again around to be reminded or tempted. If only one person would start so that others could be free. For it's only when we see face to face that true healing can begin. It's when, through the eyes of Christ, we can clearly see others and ourselves that freedom begins. So, who will be willing to go first? Will it be you or will it be me?

The Gate Keeper

As we looked through the fence, we could see the beautiful plantings and the special work that had been done. As we stood outside the gate, we just couldn't wait to get in, for each of us had waited so long. We knew the day would come when the gate would be opened, and everyone would be allowed to come in. It had taken so long up to that point that some had gotten tired from the wait and decided to move on. We though, being the few that remained, never gave up, and it was now time for us to see.

As the Gate Keeper came to unlock the gate, we noticed he had a large shiny gold key. He carefully turned the lock with the key and to us said, "Hello, we've been waiting for you." He told us He appreciated us waiting so long and informed us that even the simplest of gardens takes a lot of time, love, and patience. He told us to feel free to look around, for we were now in a place we could all call home. As we looked around, we could smell the remnant of the Holy rain and saw the footsteps of where He had been. We saw so many seats – seats that were pre-arranged. We, in amazement, walked around and couldn't believe how magnificent this place was, and how we knew the others would feel safe there. We knew He had prepared this place for us, but for us to be servants and minister to the needs of the people. We knew this place was needed, for outside the gate was a world full of hardship and pain. That so many would want a safe place to gather, and a place where they felt loved and safe. He knew it too, and that is why He prepared this place. The time had now come, for all the plantings had taken place, and everything was in bloom. There was enough of Him to go around and enough of this place to fill every heart, mind, body, and soul.

The Gatekeeper informed us about how each thing was done and placed. He described to us in great detail how it was done and for what reason it was created. There was so much to see that it was almost impossible to take it all in. Then we all felt a warm breeze and heard His voice. It was Him, the Master Gardener, and He welcomed us in. He asked if we were happy with all that had been done and if we thought it would fit – fit for everyone? We told Him it was more beautiful than we could have imagined, and we were so happy we

were now allowed in. He told us that this garden was a p
refreshing for those who needed comfort and rest. That a..., ...
someone would come to the gate, we were to quickly and gladly take
their hand and bring them joyfully in. To let them know this place
was created for them by Him. He told us to love and love some
more. To offer help and hope and most of all love beyond measure.
He told us some would stay awhile, and some would stay even
longer. That each person who would come was for a reason, and we
were to feel privileged – privileged that to them, we were called to
serve.

We knew what He had meant, for we ourselves had once been
there. We, too, had once needed that place of forgiveness, comfort,
and rest. That place where The Master Gardener and us privately
met. He told us He had equipped us with all we needed, and anytime
we needed anything, we were to call out to the Gatekeeper because
for us, He Himself was planted there.

We were then told He had to leave and prepare yet another
garden. That there had to be a garden like this in every city – a garden
created by Him for those in need. Each of us understood and gladly
walked Him to the gate and said, "See you soon" and not a goodbye,
for we knew He would be back. We were sad to see Him go but tried
to stay focused on what He had called us to do.

As we turned to come back in, the GateKeeper smiled at us, and
somehow, He looked different than before but somehow familiar. As
we studied him more closely, we knew that He the GateKeeper and
the Master Gardner were one and the same. That He really never left
us. He was here and yet also there. That even though He had to go to
prepare a garden somewhere else, He was still with us, meeting and
caring for our every need. We then felt comfort and peace and made
our way in.

Then in an instant is when we heard it – that mighty sound of
people rushing in. "Could it be so many, so soon," we thought. He,
the GateKeeper, then led us to the front, and that is when we saw the
multitudes coming and wanting in. We took those people by the hand
and joyfully ushered them in just as He said. We introduced them to
Him, the GateKeeper, and then with love, took them fully in and
showed them around. There were so many coming in that it was hard
to keep count, and yet it didn't matter, for He had said there was

more than enough to meet the need. That all we had to do was show up, and that is what we did and what we will forever do.

For now, we know we have the help and guidance of Him.

The Master Gardener and The Gate Keeper

Freedom

He thought he had won, and the victory would be his. He thought all was lost, and he'd have the last laugh. But, oh, what a shock it had to have been for him to see that from his plan you were freed.

For now, within you, there is victory and such peace of mind. Your life has been restored and brought back to your Heavenly Father, never again to go back – back to the great deceiver. For life with God always pushes you ahead into the perfect will of the Father.

Once again, a precious life has been touched and delivered. A life that now has the freedom to shine as a light and for the Father. What the enemy thought he could kill has been freed to bring life. What he planned to destroy has now been set free to bring eternal healing.

Another life freed, restored, and brought fully back. To prove once again that He, the living God is divinely faithful. To prove once again that He is more powerful than anything else that has been created. To prove once and for all that whatever would try to exalt itself above the Heavenly Father can never stand nor last.

All of this to forever prove the power and freedom of being a Christ follower and believer.

When?

What will it take to get our attention? Worse yet, what will it take to keep our attention? Will it take another natural disaster or perhaps another personal tragedy for us to see?

So often, we try and try to do things our own way, and yet it never satisfies and only lasts for so long. When will we realize that life is not about us or getting things? That life is about surrendered living in a Holy and Godly way. When do we say we are done, and we've had enough? When do we honestly admit that our good intentions are not always enough? How many falls from pride do we have to experience? How many moments of rejection do we need to be subjected to before we look to Him above? When do we finally get tired of only looking to ourselves? When do we openly admit that others will never be able to fill that empty place inside? When do we humble ourselves before Him at the Heavenly throne and sincerely repent? When do we say, "I have had enough, Lord," and before Him lay our own plans aside? When do we fully and consciously say that for ourselves, we will no longer exist?

Oh, we make it so much harder than it was intended to be. For it is because of our own choices often that we are in a deep dark pit. Yet God watches us from above and says, "When will you finally quit?" "When will you finally give it up and let me take over?" "When will you not only let me be your Savior but also your Lord?" "When will you give Me your hand letting Me pull you out, and better yet forever keep you out?" "When will you let Me be the moral compass of your life and prove to you that in Me, you can always trust?"

Only when we can humbly cry out, "Forgive me, Lord, I'm done," is when the running stops, and with Him, we daily walk. Only then can God be Father and in us do a new work. It's only then He can feed us and prepare us for the journey that lies ahead. It's only when we take our eyes off of ourselves and back at Him look that we can clearly see. It's only when we dedicate our hearts and lives to Christ that true living begins. The only thing that is left is the question:

When?

Free to Fly

While out driving one day, I noticed something trying to cross the road. As I slowed down to look, I saw that it was a small caterpillar. This tiny creature was slowly but intently inching its way across the road, undoubtedly trying to hurry amongst all the passers-by. It inched and inched itself across, not giving into the cars traveling on the other side. It was sad to watch, yet I couldn't help but wait to see if it would make it. As I sat there waiting for it to cross, I remembered what was taught to me years ago in school. I remembered how the teacher explained the process of how a caterpillar goes through the transition of turning into a perfect butterfly. I realized this small furry creature with no apparent outward beauty would one day become one of the most beautiful and free creatures that has ever been created. It may not have looked like anything magnificent then, but one day after it had been let out of its cocoon, it would forever be beautiful and around the world free to fly. I watched that caterpillar safely cross into the dirt and debris on the other side of the road and saw how quickly it blended in. I wondered where it would go and how it would survive but knew somehow it would safely find its way, and it was time for me to go.

As I then stopped at the next traffic light, I saw a beautiful purple and yellow butterfly come into my sight. This small amazing creature had landed on my windshield out of the blue and allowed me the privilege of seeing what the finished process of transition looks like, and oh, what a sight it was. I could see the beautiful markings, perfectly formed wings, and watched in amazement as its wings moved as though they were playing music. This butterfly had landed long enough for me to notice it, and then as quick as it came, it easily flew away. It was now free to fly and explore new places along with new faces. My mind then went back to the small fuzzy creature that I had just seen trying to cross the road. That creature just blended in but would one day be for all an obvious sight.

The Lord then quickly reminded me of my life. How at different times, I also had not looked so good and was just blending in. How at times, I was going so slow and just hoping I would also be able to safely cross. How also, because I was willing to go through the process of transition, I have now become like that same purple and yellow butterfly. I was able, through Christ, to survive the passers-by in my life and eventually push my way through that somewhat tightening cocoon. What I may have looked like to others at one time was not who I was intended to be. Now I'm free like that purple and yellow butterfly, and able to spread my God-given wings and freely fly. He also gently but firmly reminded me it was also because of someone else being willing to take the time and help me safely cross that I am where I'm at today. That the colors of my life should now be used to bring hope to others so that, for them, they also can be changed.

I may not totally forget every detail of who I was and what choices I had made in my past, but now it doesn't matter. I was not defined by God by what I did then, but rather by what God Himself had predestined and said. I am now in a new season of my life and able to freely fly and be all that God wants me to be. Ultimately that is to bring hope and peace into the windows of other's hearts and be a living example and testimony of God's love, mercy, and grace. To be able to bring a message of hope around the world that inspires not only hope but also change so that others will be able to freely fly. To help others see and recognize, although the process may be difficult at times, it is so worth it. To encourage people not to avoid going through that process, because it's in the process you find out who you really are and what you're made of; just like that strong caterpillar who was willing to cross the road no matter how long or how hard. He didn't give up, and because of that, he will be transformed and able to fly.

Becoming who God has intended us to be is a process, a life-changing process that requires transition. One day though, you will look back and be extremely grateful you did not give up. You will be thankful you made it, and others will be able to see what God can really do. People will look at you and say, "I can't believe the change that has taken place – what a wonderful testimony."

All of this for you to shine and fly just as God intended you too all along. So, the next time you see a perfectly formed butterfly know that it didn't start out that way as it had to first go through the process. The process that took time, perseverance and strength but was worth it because in the end it got to freely fly, and so will you.

Oh, and one last thing, remember that inside every caterpillar, there is something unique and beautiful waiting to come out – waiting to come out so it too can fly. So, when you look at yourself, know that even though you're going through the process, God is not finished with you yet, and one day you will break out and freely fly.

A Day At The Movies

Imagine one day going to the theatre with a group of your friends. Some you have known for years, and some you've just only recently met. You have all gathered together, and have found yourselves the best seats, and have finally settled in. The lights then slowly start to fade, and the screen light comes on. The announcer says that the regularly programmed movie has been canceled and that there will be a new one shown.

The crowd then begins to stir, and everyone wonders what is going on. You and your friends, though, decide to stay and watch while some of the others have decided to go on. Just then, the screen that once was white now has a picture of you on it. The images of you continue to be shown- pictures starting the day you were born. Everyone starts to "ooh," and "awe," and even out loud with you do they laugh. Then time fast forwards, and there's you involved in your first sin. Suddenly you look around and question what is going on. "How can this be?" you think as you try to escape, but there's no getting away, for you are forced to stay and watch. This time on the screen, the image you see is the one you had hoped you would one day forget. The picture you see is you yet involved in another ugly sin, and before you, they are becomingly increasing more. The sins on the screens have now been the ones you have tried so hard to hide. The others are now looking at you, not in "oohs" and "awes" anymore but in absolute disbelief. They're looking at you now, wondering why to them you have been so judgmental and hard when your yourself had also committed a sin. For the things that were on the screen were the very things about them, you had previously so quickly judged. The things on the screen that brought you shame were the things you never with them allowed yourself to discuss. Then as the movie comes to an end, the house lights come on, and your friends are now allowed to leave, and they quickly do-one by one.

You are now left alone in the theatre to sit and think about what you have done. As you quietly sit, you notice that the screen has now changed. The image that is now in front of you is Him writing something in the dirt. You now see Jesus standing with a woman at

His side, and the others across from her have cold, hard stones in their hands. They have brought her to Him accusing her of a deathly sin. Jesus then says to them that whoever is without sin are to cast the first stone. One by one, they start to leave till the only ones who were left were her and Him. Jesus then tells her to go and sin no more, and from that moment, she was free to go.

As you sit there, you now realize who and what you have become. You yourself have become like those who had those cold hard stones in their hands. You realize how many times you have held up a similar stone in front of someone even though you also had once been there. After realizing this, you in that theater kneel to your knees and humbly bow your head. You tell the lord how sorry you are and to Him repent asking for forgiveness. You then promise to not approach others with a cold hard stone in your hand, but rather choose to reach out with open and helpful hands extended to others. To show others that even though we all have sinned, we are through Christ forgiven, and no one is better than another. At that moment on your knees, you also ask the Holy Spirit to remove the hardness of your heart and to create in you a new and clean heart, and in Christ's name, you humbly pray amen.

As you then rise and look around, you see that although you are physically alone, you feel completely fulfilled. As you turn to leave, you notice that the screen again turns on, and imprinted on it is a simple one-line message that reads to you:

"Go And Sin No More."

The Perfect Meeting Place

One night out of hurt and pain, she went to the place where she had seen her grandfather so faithfully go. That special meeting place alongside the bed, and so she too went and humbly knelt on her knees. As she knelt with her hands folded, she started to pour out her heart before God, telling Him all that was on her mind and broken in her heart. She asked for forgiveness and for change to take place. Change that was not only needed for others but also the change that needed to first take place inside of her.

She wept for what seemed hours until she felt she could cry no longer and then asked for mercy and grace, and above all, His perfect strength. She told the Lord her God that in Him she was now going to fully trust. As she sat there so still, she could feel the heat of the last tear upon her face. She knew she had been broken, and that was why she was there. She knew all though so much change needed to take place, she herself was finding out who in the storm she really was. She realized that even though the storm was rough, it was a storm that needed to happen and a storm that could be ridden out with the help of her God. That even in the storm, she saw all the things inside of her that needed to be restored. For she, at times, was turning into someone she didn't know, much less like. So, to be on her knees in that moment was a moment that would change the rest of her life.

Then, when all was said and done, she lifted her head and let out a line of praise and thanksgiving to her listening and compassionate God. Even though at that moment she was feeling pain and hurt, she knew He for her had endured so much more and would see her through. She then wiped her misty eyes and finished with a thank you and an amen. She rose to her feet and somehow felt taller than before, for then she realized the weight had been lifted. She crawled into her bed, closed her tired eyes, and asked the Lord her God for protection and peaceful sleep, and then fell fast asleep.

All this taking place at the side of one woman's bed with no one looking or listening except Him, her faithful God. All of this because she chose to follow an example set from long ago and meet with her God. For now, she sees why he from long ago had so humbly knelt on his knees. For he knew, just as she now does, that on our knees before Him is always:

The Perfect Meeting Place

Vessels of Ministry

As she sat alone one night, she began to wonder why on this earth, she was planted. What purpose did she serve, and what, if any, was the call upon her life? Oh, she knew she had responsibilities, ones that she was to guide and oversee, and the daily tasks of doing the normal expected things. As she sat there, though, she began to really wonder and ponder the meaning of her life and existence. Could she, being just an ordinary woman, be called to a ministry? She had seen on tv how at different times, people would say they had been called to ministry and thought maybe it was just for them. That somehow to her, ministry only seemed to represent being a pastor or even a worldwide evangelist.

Here she was, she thought, just an ordinary woman, who had her own shares of life's ups and downs. How, at times, her life had been difficult, but then someone would come along with a similar problem, and from her pain and past, she herself would share of God and His goodness but was that considered ministry, she wondered? She asked God to show her what her life meant and what purpose did it serve for Him. She asked that He show her why she was even formed and was ministry only for those she had seen on tv. Then quickly, her mind recalled so many moments that had taken place in her life. Moments in which her neighbor needed help, and she was the first one there. The time when the church needed help in the Sunday school class, and she was able to volunteer. She remembered the relative who needed extra support and how she cheerfully went. She remembered a stranger from long ago who, when in passing, she gave a friendly smile back too. Then, the last was a teenager she once knew who had lost their way and, with her guidance, found their way home.

God, through these memories, carefully pointed out this was and is ministry. He showed her ministry is purely Godly living, sharing, and serving others. God showed her that ministry is not a title to be attained or a tv show to appear on, but it's about serving God and others. That each of us is called to some sort of ministry even if it never goes outside of our own homes. It may be defined as one thing, but often it's a matter of lifestyle that counts as a ministry. She then smiled and felt relief that even she herself, just an ordinary woman, could be in ministry. All along throughout her life, God had given her moments to reach the needs of others through His name, and that was true ministry. Upon finally realizing this, she prayed for God to grant her more moments of ministry, the grace to follow through, and above all He would always be glorified.

Now, as she sat there, she fully saw herself for what she was — a vessel of ministry. Even though she didn't understand it, she was thankful God could and had used her for the furthering of His Kingdom. Thankful that He was going to continue to use her for the ministry of others. After all, through Him, she now realized, as all of us are, that she was called, chosen, and anointed for ministry.

Adversity

Often when we're at our limit, we cry out to the one person who can bring change, and that is our God. We ask He suddenly remove all the obstacles and annoyances that seem to be right in our way. We know He hears and answers prayers, which is why we go to Him in the first place. When we're done, we believe He has answered us and positive change is on the way.

Suddenly there seems to erupt adversity coming in at every angle. Things have gone from bad to worse and now we're in amazement as to how all this could be happening. That child who once was so obedient has now chosen to be rebellious. The finances we were sure would always be there have now become shaky and unsure. The marriage that everyone has once envied is now being tested to its core. That once healthy body has now been turned over to such a deathly disease. A friend who once claimed to be forever loyal has now shown a side of betrayal. The career that seemed to be so promising has now been let go of due to downsizing. So again, we go before our God and ask, "Why – why is all this happening?" Didn't He hear our cry for help? Didn't He know the first time we came to Him, we were at our limit? How does He think we can endure this or even anymore?

Then, in a moment of quietness, God reveals to us He is doing exactly as we had asked. He is bringing change and yet even revival, just like we prayed for. The problem, though, is we are not approving of how it has come packaged. Gods say to us, "Please remain still, remembering I'm in control and know what I'm doing. In order for change and revival to be everlasting, I need to allow things to hit rock bottom in order for Me to get all the glory." He tells us, even though this was not what we have liked or wanted, it will do us some good to be refined and tested during this time. He tells us if we would just keep our focus on Him and allow change and revival to come, that even through us, there would be one more miracle added to the pile. He tells us He is aware of the hurt and pain we are going through and He will be the one who will safely see us through, and it's only temporary. He reminds us also, He does expect us in the adversity to trust Him and let Him do His perfect will. To realize that even though adversity has broken out, it had to be this way, and in the end, will prove to have been a good thing. The good thing is this was the only way to ensure change and revival would begin, and in the end, we would all win.

So, when adversity comes knocking, go ahead and answer the door. Know that although it was not what you might have prayed for, adversity will teach you some things. Those things, had it not been for adversity, you would never have learned. So, while for a moment, times may be difficult, know God sees and is aware of all things. That whatever you need to get through it, He will give to you. In the end, the change you prayed for will be an everlasting one, along with yourself as well. All because of something called:

Adversity.

The Road of Process

She knew her life was about to change and all that lay ahead and wondered if she had enough. She had the faith all along to believe in it; however, did she now have the endurance she needed to go through with it? So many times, she had wanted to give in, and so many times, she'd question if she should just stop and give up.

The Lord, though to her, had been so faithful carrying her through each stressful day. He knew the road for her had at times been long and hard. He also saw all the countless tears that behind closed doors by her were shed. He saw all the frustration that at times was upon her face and had even heard all the thoughts leading to depressing words. He knew, though, she had to travel on that long road – the road called "process." The road that at times had seemed unending. For He knew the day for her would finally come – the day when all the time in between would help her on her new road.

So, did she have what it takes, and would she make it successfully? Oh, she knew she absolutely would for why else had she been created? She was created for this very purpose, for besides family, what else is there? She had seen herself evolve over time, and now it was time to go. It was time to go and see all God had pre-planned. All the behind the scene plans that to her had once only been a mystery. For her, the road of process would prove to have been a blessing in disguise. It was because of that road; it now enabled her to freely and confidently go.

So again, did she have what it took? Oh, yes, she absolutely did, and it was something no one could ever take from her. She had found the strength before, and this was just the beginning of change. This change would start her destiny. She knew a different road for her now lay ahead. A road sometimes paved with hardships for sure, but mostly a road paved with blessings. A road she had so carefully, over time, been groomed for. The road which brings freedom to all those she would meet. The road that represents Jesus in all she would do and say. It wasn't going to be about her or even having some specialized skills, but rather it was about God Almighty helping her to fulfill her destiny. The destiny that said to millions, come to Christ and be changed and renewed. Come to Christ and experience love, forgiveness, and healing. The road that says each one has a divine pre-destined purpose. The road on which hopefully others will freely want to travel. The road where she would freely share all that had happened to her in her life. All that had happened to her on that blessed road called:

The Road of Process.

Just Wait

Can anything stop the hand of God from moving? Can anything be prevented in and of ourselves or others? God said He is the author and finisher of our faith and His word would not come back void. So, why do we worry? He said He would finish the good work He has started in us, and by seeking Him, everything else would be added.

The truth is, nothing or no one can stop the perfect will of God from becoming a reality in our lives, and no circumstance is too big for God to overcome. We ourselves are the ones who lock the Almighty into a very small box because of the belief that certain things to God are too impossible to be achieved. The only thing He asks of us is to be obedient in all things and to daily seek His face and not only his hand. To daily allow His Holy Spirit to renew and strengthen us by walking in the spirit, and to our flesh daily crucify. To trust whatever He has spoken to us will one day be a reality. To walk through the God-ordained process knowing through Him, our best interests are being handled, and nothing or no one can stop God's perfect will from becoming real. To trust when things look bleak and impossible, it is rather the beginning of change and great things to come. To fully realize God is not bound to the flesh but is working and operating in the supernatural and doesn't think or act like those of us on this earth. His ways far outweigh anything we could imagine, and above all we could ask or think He is willing to freely give us. So, we do not need to fret or worry, but rather be at perfect peace and rest knowing He sees and knows all, and for us is always working.

So, what do we need to do? We need to daily stop, look and listen to all He is trying to show and tell us, and allow Him to work in us as we patiently wait it out. For the things He's trying to make us see and understand are the very things we will need for our future journey. Then, when in an instant it is all revealed, we will be even more ready – ready to move ahead.

The charge, for now, is this: Simply trust and obey all you humble servants of the Most High God, knowing God counts you faithful. For one day soon, you'll be publicly seen and highly rewarded.

So, for now, just be patient and wait.

Are You The One?

What is the ministry, and to whom are you called? Where in the world are you meant to go, and who is the group of people you are meant to make a difference with? What is the spiritual gift that was placed upon you before you were born? Is it the gift of healing or the call of the prophetic? Will you go as a pastor, or will you go as a helping friend? Will you be the one to teach the gospel, or will you be the one who has the gift of helps? Perhaps it is to intercessory prayer you are called, that behind closed doors, God to you will reveal His needs and will.

Whatever the calling is, the time has now come for those who are willing to show up. Those who have known all along that upon their life there was placed a divine call. For now is the appointed time for the anointing to flow. The anointing of the Holy Spirit that is, to all, freely poured out. It is now time to unlock the gift inside of you that has remained quiet and dormant. The gift you thought was only something imagined in your mind. The gift that boldly says it's all about Him and sets others free. The one who has heard the voice of God and knows they are anointed, gifted, and now ready to go. Ready to face the music of those who once even said, "Don't go." It is now time for them to arise and allow the gift to work, and time to now mature and accept the Holy call. Do not delay, but arise and look to the Heavens above. For He, the Holy One, is now asking and waiting for those to boldly come forward. Those who will say, no matter the risk, they themselves want to be used. Even if at them, the world may laugh, they consider it a privilege to serve. Those who are saying they don't want to blend in anymore, for earthly time is running out and for the Kingdom of God, they must now full-time work.

These are the ones God is now looking at. For these are the ones who, like David, will stand before the giants ready to fight. Declaring in Jesus name all strongholds brought on by the evil one will now be broken and destroyed. Those who will go in Jesus' name boldly declaring He the Lord is the way. So, the question for today is only this:

Are You the One?

Qualified

You believe you can't be used because of your past abortion. You believe because of your choice; you have somehow been spiritually disqualified. Some say because years ago you went through that terrible divorce, you are now done. That you committed a horrible sin and upon you is placed eternal damnation. You believe because of your past addictions; you are not to be fully free. That because drugs were your choice, you will always be seen as an addict. You believe that because you took a life, your life will never be spared. That because you broke a commandment, there is no hope for you, and you live in despair. However, look to those written about who were imperfect. David, who committed adultery, and even Moses, who committed murder. Rahab, who everyone knew as the town prostitute, and Jacob who once was known as a crook and swindler. Abraham, who, while obedient, still chose to lie. How about Peter who said he wouldn't but did and denied three times his Lord Jesus Christ. Paul who once persecuted Christians and believed he was right. Jonah who knew his destiny, and yet from God thought he could hide, so he chose to flee.

The Bible is not a book of self-righteous hypocrites; rather, it's an example and witness that no one is perfect. That even those from long ago had a so-called shady past. That even though their decisions were bad, God Himself in them saw how great their potential. God did not look to who could qualify based on their past actions because no one could. Rather, God knew their futures, and that later became the primary focus. The Bible gives many messages, and the message is unconditional love. A love that is free from judgment. That regardless of one's bad choices, we are loved and forgiven by God Almighty, and for us, He has a plan. The Bible is not meant to give unrealistic expectations or to make people feel unworthy or that there is no hope for them, but it is to help reassure us all. Even when we've blown it knowingly, His love for us is always beyond measure. When one repents and from the Father seeks forgiveness, it is granted. The slate of their lives is forever washed clean, and they can then freely and confidently move on. Mankind, which at times included those of the church, are the ones who need to remember. That although some sins in their lives have never been made public and allowed to be seen, they were once not covered by our Lord Jesus Christ's blood.

So, do you have a plan and purpose since you have committed that sin? Does God love you and see greatness in you that by others ought to be seen? Can you be used by God, and to others to be a beacon of light? Can you be the one to bring hope that is accomplished through him?

The answer is yes, yes, and again yes, for look at those from ago. They themselves committed sins, and yet for them, God still had a plan. They were put in the Bible as an account to learn from. To show us of Gods faithfulness, love, forgiveness and divine purpose. The same is true for you, even though some may look at you and say no. You may not be written in the Bible of today, but you are written in the lamb's book of life, and when others see you, they will see Christ. Through you, they will see God, His love, forgiveness, and divine purpose, for you are a living epistle, a divinely spiritual being. God will take your past and turn the shame you felt into hope, and hurt into freedom. He will take the regret and turn it into a lifelong mission. The mission that says to all God can and will use anyone. Anyone with or without a past, for to Him it does not matter. All that matters is you show up and for Him daily live. Showing up to say I'm not defined by my mistakes, but rather by God Himself. That with God, all things are possible, and for us, He will never leave. Your life can show that forgiveness of sins is available regardless if the world says you are unworthy. Showing up just like David, Moses, and Abraham saying, use me Lord, for here I am. Here I am with yes a past, but my future to you now I give. I reached for you, and you answered, and now to others, I will freely go. All because someone long ago showed up and showed me I was never disqualified. Through imperfect people you work, and that is why you get all the glory. For it is because of you we all qualify regardless of what anyone may or may not say.

Who

Who is called to the nations? Is it you or is it I? Which one will go and to the world be God's spokesperson? Who will be the one to say the hard things, and will be willing to be un-liked? Who will go and say things in Jesus' name and in front of a crowd will dare to say, "Thus says the Lord"? Who will prophesy that the need is near and will even be willing to say, "You sir there, need Jesus Christ"?

Oh, if one would be God's chosen mouthpiece. One with fire inside, ready to proclaim that Jesus is the way. One who sees sickness and disease and from inside sees even the dark side. One who knows certain things and isn't afraid for it to be revealed and taken of.

Is it you or is it me that will so fervently go? Going into the backyard streets of life, declaring that now is the appointed time. Who will stand before a crowd and know who is addicted to what and why? One who will non-judgmentally seek healing and health to those that are lost. Who will go with power and might and full of the Holy Spirit? Who will it be? Will it be you, or will it be me?

God says open not only your heart but now open your mouth and loudly speak. Speak the things the others wouldn't be willing to publicly say. Be strong, be mighty, go in love and always let love be your driving force. Go child, and let your mouth proclaim all the God-like things to you that I will say. Go to a chosen generation and be a prophetic light. Go and in Jesus' name bring those captives home. Home where there is freedom and the ability to walk forever in the light. Be not afraid of their faces, for there are those who will at you laugh, but know your reward is not on this earth but rather is eternally with Me. For one day, while standing before Me, you will hear Me to you say, "Well done, My faithful servant, and now look behind at how many because of your willingness to speak also chose to come." All because My words to them, you were willing to speak. All because you said it is me – me that will go. Me who wants to be used and to others be Your voice. The voice that says: Repent for the time is at hand. Repent.

So again, is it you or is it me? Or perhaps it is us both.
If so, oh, what a day it will be.

Yes, I Can

Why say "I can't" when God says you can? Why say "I shouldn't" when God says you should? Why sell yourself so short when God of you thinks so highly? Why tell yourself "Never" when God says, "Now is the time."

Too often decisions are made by those around us. Those who think they know and yet don't have a clue. Those who we let define our can and cannot, and allow our minds to be shaped by what we do or don't do. However, who better to know us than our Creator above. The One who's known all along just who and what we were. The One who made us with so many possibilities and wonderful capabilities.

So, in reality, we cannot say, "No, I can't." Rather, we need to say, "If God says yes, then I most certainly can. Even though I may be nervous, I can with Christ, do all things." For how else does He get to show off if we ourselves try to take all the credit?

So, because of Him, I can, and most importantly, I will. I will set my feet ahead and do what God says I can. I will do all things through Christ and remember through Him all is possible, and above all things, God is in control and through me is working and alive.

All Because I choose to believe and Go.

The Message

The look upon her face was of pure frustration, for she was tired, hurt, lonely, and everything seemed to be going wrong. He working late every night, and her just trying to keep up. The kids needing so many things, along with all the duties of bills and a house she needed to keep up.

Who at the end of the day was there for her, she thought? Who was the one for her to encouragingly say, "Good job?" Who asked if a need of hers they could lovingly fulfill? Was anyone aware of her and what she needed? Who was she deep inside that no one seemed to notice? Who was the real woman that inside of her lived? Was she only to people a daily caregiver? Was she only to others one who would always be there? Was anybody really listening to what she had to say? Did anyone care about her dreams, or was she to others only their fulfiller?

Then in an instant, it happened- that bright light that shown at the edge of her bed with to her a message. At first, she thought she was dreaming until she audibly heard her name said out loud- "Audrey," the voice so sweetly spoke. "It is I from Heaven above. The one who looks over you and to whom I am assigned. You're a gift to and from the Father and a gift to the world. Know that your life has been set apart for such a time as this, and the Lord has sent me to tell you that it is you He is pleased with. That He also sees all the acts of love you daily perform, and that you need to know your work is never in vain. He sees all the daily chores you do and the eternal works by which you teach and live. He sent me to tell you never to give up. Know that Heaven of you is proud, and up for yourself, you are laying eternal treasure. That the dreams inside you are the ones, He is going to fulfill, but you first had to learn to serve before anything in your life could go forward. Know that God Almighty sees you, and of you is so very proud. He knows at times you have struggled, but because on Him you chose to lean, is why you have come so far. Also, know that the road ahead of you will be paved with success, and others will be reached by the dream that is placed inside of you. Continue on Audrey and find rest – rest that God's eye is on you and for you is always working."

Then the bright light was gone, and the room again became dark. Oh, how much that was needed, she thought, and how blessed for Him to her give that much-needed message. That divine visitation from above that said, "I see you, and yes, you can go on." The message that said, "Keep on going, live, and one day your dream you will also outwardly live." All out of His great love for her, did He give her that day what she needed. All because He, in His infinite power, chose to send a message of encouragement to Audrey, His daughter. All because He knew. He knew that from Him she needed that message of hope and that message to carry on. That message that was sent from above because of His great and divine love for her – His love for His daughter.

Too Busy

Doesn't anyone have time anymore to meet the needs of others? Time that says, "What can I do for you" or even offering a simple "Thank you"? For time keeps daily passing on with certain needs and requests not getting met. People claiming that they will get to it, and yet at midnight, the day starts over, and the needs again were not met. Is everyone so caught up in their own stresses that helping someone else would be too much? Too much to be able to give the encouraging words and be the helping hands? Do we only give when it's convenient? If so, then we have along the way lost the giving heart of God. Have we become so preoccupied with our own lives that we have forgotten in Christ we are considered one body and called to serve? One might even dare to say, "Where are the laborers that would say here I am, I want to be used?"

Take a moment and imagine if God was for you just too busy. Too busy to meet that little need and too frustrated to help with the larger one. Think to a moment in which He said "yes" and then later to you said, "Oh, I can't. I've got to run." Or worse yet, promised He would, but in the end never showed up. What if in His own home of comfort said, "I'm not going down there. I'm just too busy to come," and because of that, it was your life that was not spared? What if He even said, "I'm just too tired to help anymore, too tired to continue on, and the rest is now up to you?"

Where would we be today if God said, "No, I'm too busy"? Where would our lives take us if He never helped or stepped in? Perhaps now it should be, "Thank you, Father, that your always near and available to my every need, and alwaysbeing right here." Forgive me, Lord, for being too busy to be your kind, sweet voice to others. Forgive me for being too busy to be a helping hand to my neighbor. Forgive me when I take it for granted that because of you, I get to live. Help me today seek out needs – needs that even I can meet. Help me from now on to never claim to another person I'm too busy. Help me to understand when I say "yes" to them; it's really a yes to you that I say it. It's all because of You and Your love that I can say, "Here, let me help." All because You first chose, out of love for me, not to be busy, and hung on a cross as Heaven above looked on. By doing that, it signified to the world that for all of us, You are never too busy!

Life

Did He ever say we wouldn't have any problems? Did He ever say we would have a carefree life? Did He ever say our hearts would never be broken, or we wouldn't ever struggle with the issue of trust? Did He ever say life would always be joyful or that our bodies would never need healing? Did He ever say that tears by us would never be shed, or we would never grow tired and weary?

Yes, He promised us an abundant life, but He also said that with blessing, there would be persecution. Yes, He promised that through Him, our joy would be complete; however, He also said the world, like Him, would us hate. Christ never promised us a perfect fairy tale life and all we have to do was follow the yellow brick road. He never said hearts would never be wounded, but instead that He came to heal the brokenhearted.

The truth is life can be hard, confusing, and tiring at times, even for those who are of the faith. For being a child of God doesn't mean one is immune to hurt and pain. It means that being a Christ-follower ensures one they are never alone in their times of distress. The One who lives inside of them is Christ, and for them is always working.

So, while He never promised us a perfect fairy tale, He did tell us in all things He is the One who would always be with us. That while things at times may be hard, He is the One who for us has and is the answer, being aware of everything we face. While the enemy is alive and out for us, through Him, we are victors, and all things are possible. While life may have its hard times, it is through Christ we have our wellbeing. Being Christ's child means all things are made available to us, and all we have to do is ask, and most of all, believe.

So, on this journey of life, I will trust and believe in my Lord and Savior, knowing He is the One who is in control and in His hands my life, future, and eternity are secure. As I awake each day, I will choose to face life with courage, joy, love, and most of all, faith. Faith that my Lord and Savior is again for me always working, and no matter what comes my way, I know that Him and I will face it together. This is what I choose to daily believe as I live out the rest of my life.

That Day

What did He think the day they laid the cross upon His back? What do you think He said when they insisted someone else help? Do you think He thought it to be too much? Do you think He wished He'd never taken part?

Do you think the pain was more in His heart or on His back? Do you think it was His body that ached or worse yet, His soul? Do you think the weight was more than He could bear, or was it all the stares? Do you think halfway up, He wanted to take it off? Do you think in that moment He wished He had never been born for this? How about the blood that poured from every inch of His body? Do you think He regretted each drop that happened to fall to the ground? What about the flesh that from Him so loosely fell?

Do you think with each blow He wished to take it all back? How about the pain from the long piercing steel nails? Do you think with each hammer strike He wished to declare it all over? How about Him seeing the pain upon His dear Mother's face? The one who He so dearly loved – do you think in that moment He wished none of it so? As He hung in high plain view, do you think He regretted His choice? His choice to be beaten, mocked, flogged, and so cruelly crucified? Do you think He would do it all over again? Do you think that just for you, He would again give His life?

Oh, the love of Christ one cannot truly fathom. For the love He displayed that day upon the cross, you and I cannot understand. Most certainly, He would, again and again, die if needed for you and for I. However, the price has been paid, and now we all can be free, Holy, and sanctified. We now have the freedom to be in eternity and with Him one day live. That is why He chose willingly that day the nails, the crown, and the cross upon the hill. All out of His deep and passionate love for us all – His love for His children.

So, as to what He thought that day as He was led to the place upon the hill. Truly, He thought of you and I. That is what was on His mind that day and still is today.

Just Believe

Was it going to be just another day – another day of the same? A day in which nothing changed either for good or for the bad. Was today a day in which she was again going to have to believe? Believe that as long as she hoped, all things would eventually be? She was tired of doing the same thing every day; praying, fasting, and hoping this was going to be the day, and yet nothing ever seemed to change. So, she sat and pondered as to what she should do. Should she quit and give up? After all, it seemed not to be working. Prayer after prayer, she prayed along with shedding so many tears. Did she have what it took to daily continue? Was it worth all the confessions of faith? After all, people by now of her no longer knew what to believe?

Then in a sudden instant is when she met Him. He came in as a bright light with such a gentle, mighty force. He now commanding the room for her upmost attention. He asked as to when it was she thought faith was lost? She, in now uttermost speechless silence, could not one word utter. She then knelt upon her knees, and so quickly bowed her head. He so gently but forcefully told her to arise and stand. To stand upon her feet and hear what the Lord would to her say. He said to her that even as Daniel had set his mind to understand, so had she. That while others said no wait, she said time is now running out. That while she thought her prayers were strictly in vain, they weren't. That each prayer along with each tear was by Him heard and in Heaven stored. That now at last, God had commanded that he come to her with a message. The message of all is well and that all for you is a go. That because she had remained faithful, He to her would now show off. That because she chose to obey, He now to others would her vindicate. That because she dared to hope against hope even like Abraham, she now had His stamp of approval and would to the world be sent and able to go.

Then before he left her, he looked so lovingly into her eyes and so tenderly and gently said, "The Father has spoken these simple words toward to you. Words that you must always hold near, trust and remember. The words to you, my dear child are simply, you must believe. Believe in who you are and whose you are. Believe in Him whom has now sent you. Believe in miracles and answered prayers. Lastly, remember all that is needed from here on out is that you continue to just simply:

Believe

The Reflection

Who is it you see when in the mirror you look? Do you see where you are now or only where you have been? Do you see all the changes that need to be made, or do you see yourself as Christ's child?

Are you willing to at yourself smile, knowing He above is doing the same? Are you willing to look in the mirror and realize God's not finished with you yet? Are you willing to see destiny instead of only past failures? Are you willing to look ahead and stop looking behind? Are you willing to say, "Here I am, send me"? Are you willing to allow yourself to even be destined for greatness? Are you willing to take mistakes and turn them into testimonies of God's mercy and grace? Are you willing to finish the race on top and not in last? Are you willing to step out of your shallow box? If you are, then look out for life is about to begin. Life that brings hope and change to not only you, but also to them. The life that says, "I'm forgiven, and now where do I begin?" The life that says, "I'm free to be who I really am. Free to be and have all He has predestined for me."

So, the next time you look in the mirror, know your life has meaning and purpose. Know that through Christ, all has been forgiven. Know it's His mercy and grace you will forever follow. Look in the mirror and see not only you but Him. Him that through you will be a Holy ignited fire. A reflection of mercy, grace, and the ability and strength to win. To win triumphantly over the one who once said you were no good.

Look now in the mirror and see you who were made in His Holy image. You who has a pre-destined plan to bring others to the throne. You are loved and highly favored by your faithful King and Creator. You are clothed in royalty and will someday wear a crown. You who when God looks at sees the beauty that's in and out. You who when God thinks about thinks of the great love He has for you.

So, hold your head high and smile and, most of all, joyously live. Know your past is your past and is eternally forgotten. Smile and live, oh precious Holy Child, for your Redeemer has set you free. Free from past transgressions and upon you has poured out love and grace. Take a closer look next time at who it is you see. Look and be thankful that it's Him whom, through you, others will see. You who are a beautiful reflection of our Savior and King.

Her Choice

As she lay alone in bed one night, she felt the need and urge to pray. Not really knowing what to say but knowing something had to be said. She lay alone and thought of herself and her life. Her now facing so many issues and wondering what would be said. She thought of God and how she loved Him and has loved Him her entire life. She thought of how He had always been with her wherever life had taken her. For her life throughout the years had gone through so many changes. Changes of choices made for her and yet choices she herself had made. Choices that forced her to choose between what she knew to do and what she wanted to do. Much to her deep sadness, she remembered how she made so many choices she knew were wrong and had ultimately brought her so much pain and regret.

Now here she was again needing His help. She needed help and, above all, mercy, and it was to her loving, faithful, and forgiving God that she cried out. She lay in bed that night, and as she thought about everything, all she could do was at first cry. Cry for the choices that were made and the choices that had come between her and her God. She repented, even on life's teetering fence – teetering as to which side to fully go into.

So that night, she chose to step in – into God's side and to do it whole heartily. She repented, asked for forgiveness, and that night re-dedicated and fully committed her life to Christ. She gave Him total control over her and her life, and vowed to do things according to His word. To live her life being completely sold out to Jesus Christ, and to take a stand in doing what is right. To take a stand even if to her, it meant she would stand alone. She chose that night to forever listen to Him, that still small voice. To listen to the One who about her knew and loved all things. She chose that night to lay down her fears, guilt along with the shame – the shame of her ugly past. She chose that night to believe in the word and not in the world. She chose and vowed to one day, even for others, be the one to make a difference. She chose that whatever would try to come against her, she and Him would, from then on, would face it together. She chose to truly believe for once and all she was loved, forgiven, and to listen to the voice of the One that was of her calling. The voice which said she was special and to His kingdom was so very much needed. All this night, she lay in her bed and prayed a heartfelt prayer – the night she chose Him.

My One Day

If you could have just one day to go wherever you wanted, where would it be? Would it be to the mountains or to the hills that you would go? Would it be to the seas or up in the sky you would dare to venture? For me, the answer is simple – I would go to Heaven. That is where I would go, even for just one day.

I'd go and see all that was there and what was being done. I'd say hello to friends and hug those long-lost loved ones. I'd walk on the streets of gold and listen to all that Moses would have to say. I'd sit and listen to how it really had been for Noah and his family, and then learn from the greats like Paul and the rest. I'd listen to all the stories the others didn't have time to tell. I would take a nap in the fields of lilies and bask in the warmth of the sun. I would enjoy not feeling any stress or anxiety and see even in amazement at how my body no longer ached but was instead finally radiant.

Then in the midst of it all, I'd go to the one who had been calling my name. The One, who before time existed, about me knew all things. I'd go with Him and listen to every word He would say. I'd listen as He would teach me and again bask in the warmth of the Son. I'd ask so many questions and tell Him openly all that would be on my mind, including my fears. I'd tell Him of how much love I had for Him and then thank Him for taking my place that day. Then upon my knees, I would even fall and ask to kiss the nail-pierced scars that were upon Him placed for me.

At the end of the day, when my time would be over, I know that even in Heaven, I would start to cry. I would cry for how happy I was that I finally got to see – see the place being prepared for me. Happy I got to see and meet so many that day and again reunited by those who I had lost. I'd cry for so many different reasons, and above all, for just one day, I got to see and be with Him- Him who for me had made a way.

I imagine I would then turn around to say goodbye and would hear, "Don't say goodbye, for we will meet again." I would then see all who were there that day smiling at me, and I would have to say, "Yes, until we meet again." I would, at that time, look at my Lord and Savior and say, "Thank you for a great day and for letting me in.

Thank you that You came and took my sins away so the next time I'm here, we will never have to say until we meet again – for then it will be forever."

If for one day I could go anywhere, that is where I would go and what I imagine it to be like – even for just one day!

Friends

It was getting late when she finally arrived. Her being so busy with the other, she wondered if there would be enough time to do all that was needed and expected? So many details left to figure out, and she again wondered if and how it would all work out.

As she arrived, she saw the tables, chairs, and all the places that had been set. So much of what needed to be accomplished had already by them been done. She couldn't believe how it all looked – everything in amazement looked above and beyond. Feeling a sense of relief and gratitude, she felt herself start to cry. Crying for how wonderful her friends to her had been and for her burden they chose to carry. They had known everything that had been going on and just how tired and worn out she had been. They had known of her loneliness and pain – the pain only some can say they themselves have been through. So, as she stood there with tears still welling in her eyes, she saw her friends for who they really were inside. She had known them all so long, and yet even that night of them was she surprised.

While standing in amazement, they all around her started to come – coming forward with their love and hugs. They each put an arm around her and started telling her how much love for her they had. Then the one in the crowd who believed in the power of prayer started to their mutual God cry out. She asked God for help, strength, wisdom, and joy for their special dear friend. That God would of her life bless, just as to so many others she had been. Then the ripple effect began, and before it was over, every woman for their friend had said a prayer. As the last amen was spoken, she looked up and so sincerely said, "Thank you for being my friend – all of you. Thank you for showing up tonight and helping me. Thank you for showing the true love and nature of Jesus Christ and for uplifting me in prayer." She then got up and started helping in preparing the room for all that had yet to take place. The room quickly filled with laughter and smiles as people took their places and again got busy. As she looked around at everyone, she thought for sure she was seeing angels, for she knew her friends were indeed from and of God. She, then looking up, said, "Thank you for my Godly friends Father and how they have been there for me. Help me to be just like them and for someone else always be willing to show up, and to just be a friend!

Him

He knew his life was coming to an end, and that's when he called her in. He told her again of all the love for her he had. That she was the light in his life, and with her, he was glad he got to live. They sat and talked for what seemed like hours, and then they knew their time had come to an end. She knew, along with him, they had to for a time depart. He on his way to his heavenly home and her left to go back to their earthly one. They now would have to spend some time apart, and even for him knowing where he was going was on him, still hard. They laughed, hugged, and said goodbye and that their love would always remain alive.

As she left and heard the door behind her close, she knew this was it. As she made her way down the long hallway, she realized for this she was not very strong. She felt tired and weak, and suddenly all alone, for now, she realized it would not the two of them be. Oh, deep inside, she knew she was not really alone, for she had Christ, but yet her heart because of losing him was broken inside. She stopped, paused, and took a breath, and prepared herself for what was ahead. The memories the two of them had made would always be in her head, and now for that she was glad. She just now had a new life to live, and sadly it didn't include him. She prayed to her God Almighty, who, because of him, she had met and asked that He would now be her best friend. She asked that for each step in her life, He would now help guide, and even of her broken heart mend.

As she left and heard the door behind her close, she almost had a grin. She knew he was now indeed gone, and with their God was walking hand in hand. She knew his soul was gone and nothing more of him on earth remained, and for that she also mourned but was glad. She looked up to the sky, and with tears streaming down her face said, "I love you, and together again, we will someday be. Tell Jesus hello, and even of Him I can't wait to someday see." Then the sun seemed to shine even warmer and brighter, and while feeling the heat, she knew it was him – her father and her best friend, and that together they would all someday be!

The Walk

She wondered where it was they were going as He led her by His hand. He not saying too much, only what He felt was needed. As they walked, she noticed the trees were again changing. Some were orange, yellow, green and some a pretty red. She could also hear the songs the birds were singing and even noticed a few butterflies flying by them. She felt as they were walking that there had been a shift in the weather, and she knew there lie ahead a new season. As they continued walking, she couldn't help but ask, "Where is it that we are going?" He, having a firm but gentle grip on her hand, did not say where it was except that it is was not where she had been.

Then He to her so softly yet intently said, "Life now for you will begin anew. You have walked a road at times that has been paved with much suffering, and yet faithful to Me you have been. Even in times of wondering when it would all end, the tears you have shed and those you so bravely held back have I of you seen. I've seen the mask of even keeping it all together when inside you wanted to cave and break. I've seen the faith by which you have successfully led. The faith that said, "This to will end." I've heard the words of encouragement – words by Me that were needed to be said in and out of season. I've seen the tearing down of pride replaced by the walls of humility. I've seen your perseverance and strong stance while striving for a higher standard when even that was not popular. To tell you the truth, child, I've seen it all. I've seen all that you've had to endure and how hard you have strived to follow through. So, as to where we are going, I'm leading you to a new place – a new journey. A place that is not paved with suffering but with reassurance, validation, and victory. I'm firmly taking your hand and leading you into a life of change. A life full of places you've never seen and experiences you thought you would never find. I'm taking you to a new road – a road that is only marked for you."

We then stopped for a moment and took in the scenery around us. Everything crisp, cool and lovely sounding as if it were all new. He at that time took both of my hands in His and said, "For now, you must go. You must take all you have learned and yet, in turn, give it away. Take your story and mended heart, and again give it away.

Don't live in the past, child, but remember the roads that led you to here, and again give it away. Fear not what others may say, for it is I who have already been there, and I who know you will be fine." Then He took my hands and upon them placed a kiss and looked up to Heaven and said, "Upon this child do now bless" and then to me He said, "Now freely go."

As I looked ahead, I almost didn't want to go for fear of the known and the unknown. He, though, of course knowing all things, again said, "Now freely go." He also reminded me I would never be alone. He would always be guiding and directing me, and my ways He would always be preparing. So, looking ahead, my mind started to fill with excitement, and I knew it was up to me. It was up to me to take the first step, and yet I still wasn't sure. He looked at me and said, "Even though you must take the first step, child, know that without Me, you will never be. I'm always here walking with and beside you, and together we will always be."

So, with confidence that day, I stepped out with Him and took the step to what lay ahead – all of this on the day He to me said, "Come, let's take a walk."

Fear Not!

Wondering if this was the beginning, she started to ask the question. The question of who would do what, and where they would all go? Would everything be as she pictured it in her mind, or would it be even bigger than she had imagined? So many questions and yet so little time, as least that's how she felt.

People starting to get antsy and knowing time was running out, and she herself just standing back and choosing to watch. She chose to watch and see, for if it was true, then what did it mean for her? Did it really mean her life was about to change, and if so, then what did that even mean? Again, so many questions and yet so few answers, at least that's what she thought. She knew this day would eventually come, and now she wondered if she, in fact, was ready for it. Was she the one who, for them, would help lead? Was she the one, with her life and testimony, to the world would go and tell? Was this the moment she had been so carefully groomed and prepared for by her heavenly father? Was this the moment in time where everyone would finally see the hand of the Lord hath done this thing and not her? Was this the time in her life when everything for the better would be brought about by change? Part of her said she hoped so, and honestly, a part of her said, "No, not yet, for I'm not ready. Please give me some more time – time to know what it is exactly that of me is expected."

Then in the gentle way the Lord of heaven will talk and push us ahead, He to her said – "This is it child, do not be afraid. Do not worry about what the others will say, for it is I who has done this divine thing. It is I who has ordained not only your every step but also you yourself. For within you, since you were a small child, have I lived and reigned, and because of that, you have moved ahead. Fear, not the role you think is required of you, for it is I who has made the way possible and deep down you know it's true, and you know with Me you can do this thing."

Upon hearing this, she knew she had a choice to make – the choice which would change the course of her life forever if she said yes. A choice that would take her out of her comfort zone, and the choice to others that would eventually bring healing and freedom because of who it was that indeed in her lived. So, with her head bowed and so quietly speaking, she with her lips whispered, almost quivering, "Yes."

She said she would do whatever would be required of her. That even though she didn't know all the details, she had faith and trust that for her, He would work all things out. Then again, she heard that quiet voice speak back to her saying, "All I want and need you to do is what you've done all along, and that is serve, serve and again serve. To go and meet the needs of the people by telling them your story and all you have learned from Me. This is all I require of you child, and with Me as your Father and partner, deep down know you are never alone and can never go wrong. So dear child, from now on go and:

Fear Not!

Praying Wives and Mothers
MINISTRIES
Small Groups • Large Impact • Spreading Hope

Praying Wives and Mothers Ministries is a place where women can safely learn their value and the love the Father has for them. A place where women can globally connect through the power of prayer and be the women God has designed them to be.

Complete List of Books Available on Amazon:

Gardens Of Splendor
God's Garden
God's Garden Tools
Help I'm A Leader
Now What?
The Godly Gatekeeper
The Noble Woman
Seed For The Sower
Sitting With The Master Gardener

To learn more, visit our website.

www.prayingwivesandmothersministries.org
gina@prayingwivesandmothersministries.org